The Comic Strip
ODYSSEY

THE COMIC STRIP

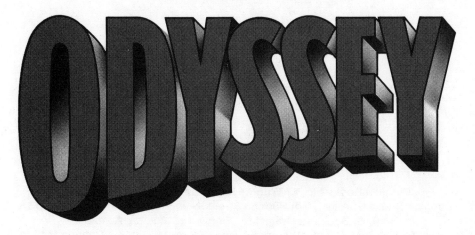

ODYSSEY

Homer's classic,
retold in words and pictures by

DIANE REDMOND
and
ROBIN KINGSLAND

VIKING

To our friends at the Polka, with love

VIKING

Published by the Penguin Group
Penguin Books Ltd, 27 Wrights Lane, London W8 5TZ, England
Penguin Books USA Inc., 375 Hudson Street, New York, New York 10014, USA
Penguin Books Australia Ltd, Ringwood, Victoria, Australia
Penguin Books Canada Ltd, 10 Alcorn Avenue, Toronto, Ontario, Canada M4V 3B2
Penguin Books (NZ) Ltd, 182-190 Wairau Road, Auckland 10, New Zealand

Penguin Books Ltd, Registered Offices: Harmondsworth, Middlesex, England

First published 1992
Based on the play written by Diane Redmond, first performed at the Polka
Children's Theatre, Wimbledon, London, in 1990
1 3 5 7 9 10 8 6 4 2

Text copyright © Diane Redmond, 1992
Illustrations copyright © Robin Kingsland, 1992

The moral right of the author and illustrator has been asserted

Printed in England by Clays Ltd, St Ives plc

A CIP catalogue record for this book is available from the British Library

ISBN O-670-83661-3

WHO'S WHO IN THE COMIC STRIP ODYSSEY

GREEKS

Odysseus, King of Ithaca
Penelope, his wife
Telemachus, their son
Eurylochus) Officers in
Polites) Odysseus' army

GODS

Zeus, greatest of the gods
Hermes, messenger of the gods
Poseidon, the sea god
Athene, goddess of wisdom
Calypso, a lesser goddess
Circe, a witch and a lesser goddess

MONSTERS

Polyphemus, the Cyclops
The Sirens
The Lotus Eaters
Scylla, the six-headed monster
Charybdis, the whirlpool

OTHERS

Alcinous, King of the Phaeacians
Aeolus, King of Aeolia
Eumaeus, a swineherd and loyal servant of Odysseus
The Suitors
Argos, Odysseus' dog
The Soul of Tiresias, a blind prophet

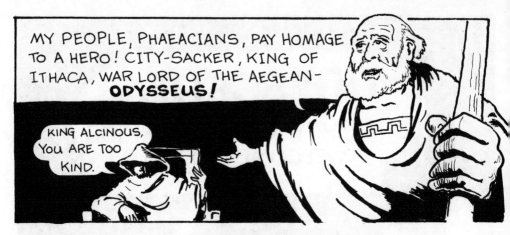

...THEN TELL ME,

COULD ODYSSEUS DO.....

THIS!?!

ER....ER.... I RECKON HE COULD. PLEASED TO MEET YOU, GREAT HERO. (Grovel grovel)

SIT DOWN, BOY, AND I'LL TELL YOU A TALE OF HEROES....

FROM THE DAY OUR WOODEN HORSE WAS WHEELED INTO TROY, VICTORY WAS OURS!

THAT!

THE LUMBERING, ONE-EYED MONSTER HERDED IN HIS SHEEP, SHEEP AS BIG AS HORSES, AND I, LIKE A FOOL, SPOKE OUT.

...GIVE ME THOSE WINESKINS, RIGHT NOW! COME ON, STACK THEM UP IN THE CORNER. **QUICK! MOVE!**

WINE! AT A TIME LIKE THIS?

DON'T MOCK. ODYSSEUS IS CUNNING. HE'S GOT A PLA...

THIS SHOULD KEEP THE CYCLOPS HAPPY.

GREAT GOD! WINE - TO SHARPEN YOUR DIVINE APPETITE.

WINE, ER?

MMM I LIKES WINE

BETWEEN COURSES.

THE MONSTER DRANK. AS QUICKLY AS HE DRAINED ONE WINESKIN I HANDED HIM ANOTHER, AND ANOTHER, AND ANOTHER! FINALLY, HE WAS BLOTTO!

AAAARR

KILL HIM!

REVENGE POLYPHEMUS, SON OF POSEIDON.

BOOM
BOOM
BOOM
BOOM
BOOM

HERE WE ARE, POLYPHEMUS.

BOOM
BOOM
BOOM
BOOM
BOOM

WHO HURT YOU?

BOOM
BOOM
BOOM
BOOM
BOOM
BOOM

WE'LL CATCH HIM AND KILL HIM.

NOBODY! HE HURT ME. HE BLINDED ME. CATCH HIM. **KILL** NOBODY

HUH! WHO'S NOBODY?

KILL NOBODY. THAT'S IMPOSSIBLE!

NOBODY? HE'S OFF HIS HEAD.

HAS BEEN FOR YEARS.

COME ON, HE'S WASTING OUR TIME.

NOBODY INDEED

HE'S DRUNK.

SLEEP IT OFF, POLYPHEMUS.

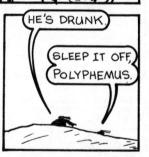

WAIT!

WHERE ARE YOU GOING? NOBODY'S ESCAPING.

IDIOT! GO BACK TO BED.

NOBODY! HO! HO! HO!

TATTERED AND TORN, WE STEERED OUR BLASTED SHIP ACROSS THE WINE-DARK SEAS —

AND CAME AT LAST TO THE LAND OF KING AEOLUS.

HERE WE FOUND REAL HOSPITALITY AND TIME TO REBUILD OUR BATTERED SHIP. THEN WE TURNED OUR EYES EAST, TO ITHACA. BEFORE WE LEFT, KING AEOLUS GAVE ME A PARTING GIFT.

NOBODY TOUCHES THIS BAG BUT **ME!**

IPPED ABOUT BY THE WINDS OF THE WORLD, WE WERE BLOWN ACROSS THE AEGEAN – THE REMNANTS OF A ONCE MIGHTY CREW.

ODYSSEUS!

ODYSSEUS!

WHERE ARE MY MEN?

PIGS! I'M NOT TELLING PORKIES, CAP'N. THE WITCH HAS TURNED THEM INTO P-P-PIGS!

TAKE ME THERE — NOW!

T-T-TAKE YOU THERE?

NO, CAP'N, PLEASE. DON'T MAKE ME GO BACK.

SHE'LL HAVE OUR BACON!

THEN I'LL GO, ALONE.

BU...BU...BUT.

MY MEN NEED ME. WAIT HERE.

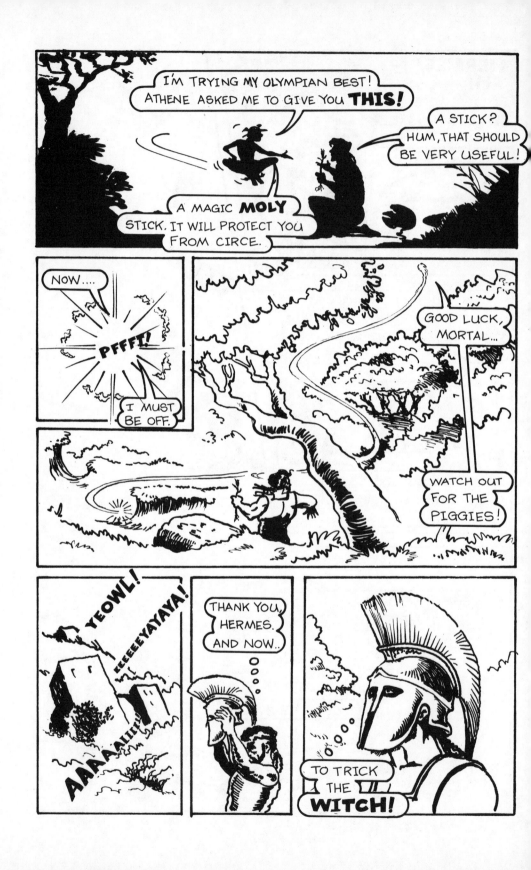

WITH MY MEN BESIDE ME AND THE MOLY IN MY HAND, I WAS STRONGER THAN CIRCE. MY POWER MADE HER LOVE ME. SHE GAVE US FOOD AND WINE AND BEFORE I KNEW IT I WAS POURING OUT ALL MY TROUBLES....

I NEVER WANTED A LIFE LIKE THIS. FIFTEEN YEARS I'VE BEEN FIGHTING AND WANDERING. I WANT TO GO HOME! I WANT TO SEE MY WIFE AND SON. I WANT A QUIET LIFE FOR ZEUS'S SAKE!

YOU'RE NOT USING YOUR HEAD, ODYSSEUS. **THINK!**

THINK **WHAT?**

WHOSE CITY DID YOU DESTROY?

POSEIDON'S

WHOSE SON DID YOU BLIND?

POSEIDON'S

WHO HAS THE POWER OVER THE WIND AND THE SEA?

POSEIDON!

OF COURSE! BUT HOW CAN I FIGHT A GOD?

THE GODDESS ATHENE PROTECTS YOU, MORTAL. YOU SAW HER POWER OVER ME. PERHAPS SHE CAN OUTWIT THE SEA GOD.

I NEED ADVICE WHO CAN GUIDE ME OUT OF THIS MESS?

TIRESIAS.

I'LL GO TO HIM RIGHT NOW.

NOT SO HASTY, GREEK. TIRESIAS LIVES IN HADES, IN THE VALLEY OF THE SHADOWS. DO YOU HAVE THE COURAGE TO TRAVEL TO HELL AND BACK?

DO I REALLY HAVE ANY CHOICE?

HAVE YOUR CREW AND YOUR SHIP READY AT DAWN. I WILL GUIDE YOU TO HELL AND YOUR CUNNING WILL BRING YOU BACK!

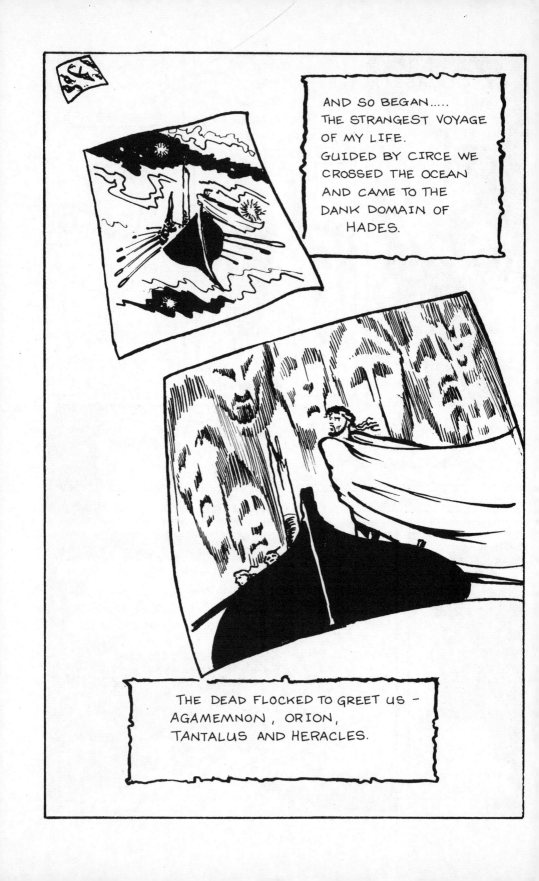

AND SO BEGAN.....
THE STRANGEST VOYAGE
OF MY LIFE.
GUIDED BY CIRCE WE
CROSSED THE OCEAN
AND CAME TO THE
DANK DOMAIN OF
HADES.

THE DEAD FLOCKED TO GREET US —
AGAMEMNON, ORION,
TANTALUS AND HERACLES.

CIRCE HAD INDEED TOLD ME ABOUT THE SIRENS AND THEIR BEAUTIFUL SONG. HOW IT DRIVES MEN MAD AND SENDS THEM RUNNING TO THEIR DEATH.

THE SIRENS TRAP THEIR PREY AND KILL THEM, SLOWLY STRIPPING THE FLESH FROM THEIR BONES. THESE BEAUTIFUL MAIDENS ARE DEADLY MONSTERS!

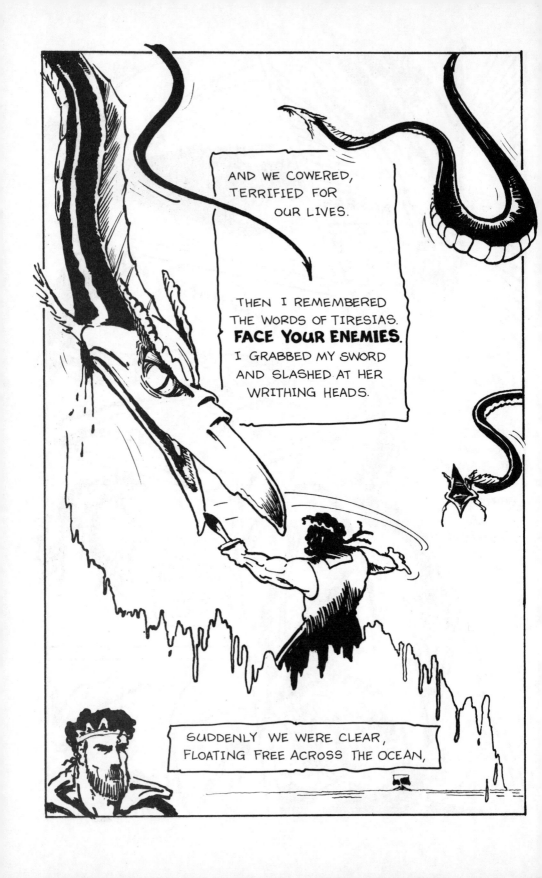

LEAVING SCYLLA AND CHARYBDIS FAR BEHIND.

FOR DAYS WE DRIFTED, BATTLE-WORN AND STARVING. THEN WE CAME TO AN ISLAND WHERE CATTLE GRAZED IN ROLLING MEADOWS.

NOTHING ON EARTH CAN SAVE YOUR MEN, ODYSSEUS. THEY WILL DIE. BUT YOU CAN LIVE, IF YOU LEAVE NOW. SWIM, RUN, WALK ON WATER - JUST GET AWAY, **NOW!**

BUT I CAN'T LEAVE WITHOUT MY MEN.

THEN JOIN THEM IN HADES.

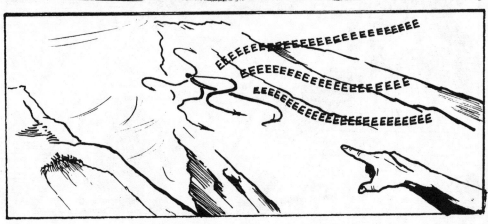

A MIGHTY WAVE PICKED ME UP AND HURLED ME AT THE CLIFFS. INSTEAD OF HITTING ROCK...

HAH!

MY FINGERS GRASPED THE BRANCHES OF A TREE.

ALL DAY LONG I HUNG FROM THAT FIG TREE, LIKE A BAT, WATCHING CHARYBDIS SUCK AND SPEW OUT THE PITIFUL REMAINS OF MY BATTLESHIP.

I WAS WAITING,

WAITING FOR MY MOMENT,

KNOWING THAT

TIMING

WAS **EVERYTHING.**

I CAUGHT CHARYBDIS AS SHE SPEWED OUT THE LAST TIMBERS OF MY WARSHIP. CLINGING TO THE BROKEN MAST, I BOWED MY HEAD AND SLEPT.

WHEN I AWOKE I WAS ON THE ISLAND OF CALYPSO. THE GODDESS FOUND ME AND FELL IN LOVE WITH ME. SHE KEPT ME PRISONER THERE FOR TEN LONG YEARS.

TEN YEARS!

EVERY DAY I STOOD ON THE SHORE AND WEPT FOR ITHACA BUT NOTHING MOVED CALYPSO,

NOTHING **MORTAL** ANYWAY.

HERMES! WHAT MESSAGES DO YOU BRING TODAY?

PING!

ONE TO FREEZE YOUR HEART, GODDESS. YOU MUST RELEASE ODYSSEUS.

NO! NEVER!

ATHENE PROTECTS HIM AND ZEUS, HER FATHER, ROLLS THE CLOUDS. FREE ODYSSEUS, OR DISPLEASE THE MIGHTY ONE.

IT'S WHAT WE GODS CALL A NO-WIN SITUATION.

THEN I MUST FREE MY LOVE?

EXACTLY. ANY MESSAGES TO THE OLYMPIANS?

YES.

TELL THEM TO KEEP THEIR OLYMPIAN NOSES OUT OF **MY** BUSINESS!

PING!

I'LL TELL THEM. FAREWELL!

POSEIDON STIRRED UP THE SEA AND HURLED ME AT THE ROCKS. TIME AND AGAIN I SMASHED AGAINST THEM, MY FINGERS GRASPING FOR A HOLD.

WHEEEEE!

WISDOM! WHERE ARE YOU NOW?

NOBLY SAID
MY FRIEND.
GIVE ME
YOUR HAND

HOORAY!

HOORAY!

I ......

OH!
MY LORD.

HE'S
COLLAPSED!

POOR MAN,
HE'S HALF
DEAD.

GO, PREPARE
THE SHIP.
WE'LL TAKE
HIM HOME
TONIGHT.

I ENTERED THE CITY, A STRANGER IN MY OWN LAND, ONLY ARGOS RECOGNIZED ME. AFTER TWENTY YEARS HE RAN INTO MY ARMS, AND DIED THERE.

ROWF! ROWF!

?

I DON'T BELIEVE IT!

EVEN LIKE THIS YOU RECOGNIZE ME, EH, ARGOS OLD DOG!

HYYYYYNNNN!

THERE... THERE...

JUST TWO OLD WARRIORS GOING GREY TOGETHER, EH, BOY? EH, ARGOS?

GOODBYE, ARGOS. GOODBYE, MY OLD FRIEND.

HIS OLD HEART STOPPED FOR EVER.

PRINCE TELEMACHUS, EUMAEUS THE SWINE-HERD IS HERE WITH A STRANGER.

TELEMACHUS, MY SON.

YOUR **SON!** MY FATHER'S DEAD AND YOU MUST BE NINETY IF YOU'RE A DAY.

EUMAEUS, SHOW THIS OLD MAN OUT.

WAIT!

NOT SO HASTY, BOY.

I'VE GOT SOMETHING TO SHOW YOU.

NOW DO YOU RECOGNIZE ME?

SWEET GODS!

YOU **ARE** MY FATHER.

ATHENE DISGUISED ME SO THAT I COULD ENTER MY PALACE AND SEE THE CHANGES BROUGHT ABOUT BY THESE DOGS!

THE SUITORS.

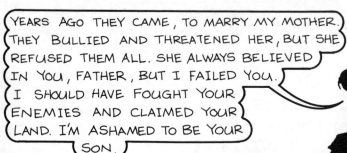

YEARS AGO THEY CAME, TO MARRY MY MOTHER. THEY BULLIED AND THREATENED HER, BUT SHE REFUSED THEM ALL. SHE ALWAYS BELIEVED IN YOU, FATHER, BUT I FAILED YOU. I SHOULD HAVE FOUGHT YOUR ENEMIES AND CLAIMED YOUR LAND. I'M ASHAMED TO BE YOUR SON.

TELEMACHUS! YOU WERE A BOY, BUT NOW YOU'RE A MAN.

COME, TOGETHER WE WILL DRIVE THE ENEMY OUT.

FATHER!

LET THEM THINK I AM A POOR BEGGAR.

THEN WE'LL **STRIKE!**

DO NOT TELL YOUR MOTHER WHO I AM. FIRST WE'LL RID MY PALACE OF THIS FILTH, THEN WE'LL CELEBRATE.

YOU'RE A GREAT WARRIOR, FATHER, BUT THERE ARE ONLY TWO OF US AGAINST THIS RABBLE.

TELEMACHUS, FOR TWENTY YEARS I HAVE OUTWITTED GODS, MEN AND MONSTERS. YOU DON'T THINK THAT I WOULD RUN AWAY FROM THESE FOOLS.

LISTEN...

LATER

GENTLEMEN!

MY MOTHER, PENELOPE, QUEEN OF ITHACA, WISHES TO SPEAK TO YOU.

MY LORDS. FOR TWENTY YEARS I HAVE REFUSED A HUSBAND, BELIEVING IN MY HEART THAT ODYSSEUS LIVED.

I CAN NO LONGER CLING TO THAT DREAM.

CHOOSE ME, QUEEN, I'LL MAKE YOU HAPPY.

WHOOPEE!

YEH, BETTER OFF WITH THE LIVING THAN THE DEAD.

COO-EEE! I'M OVER HERE. COME AND GET ME HIC!

WAIT!

I HAVE ARRANGED A TEST, A SHOW OF STRENGTH. HERE IS ODYSSEUS'S GREAT BOW. ONLY THE MIGHTIEST OF WARRIORS CAN STRING IT. IF ANY MAN HERE CAN BEND THE BOW, AND STRING IT, THEN I SHALL TAKE HIM FOR MY HUSBAND.

GIVE IT HERE.

PIECE OF CAKE.

LET'S HAVE A GO.

TWANG!

WOW!

INCREDIBLE! HOWD'YA DO THAT?

PRETTY GOOD, MATE.

GENTLEMEN...

WHO ARE YOU?

ALLOW ME TO INTRODUCE MYSELF.

AH!

ZEUS! IT'S HIM!

ULP!

ODYSSEUS!

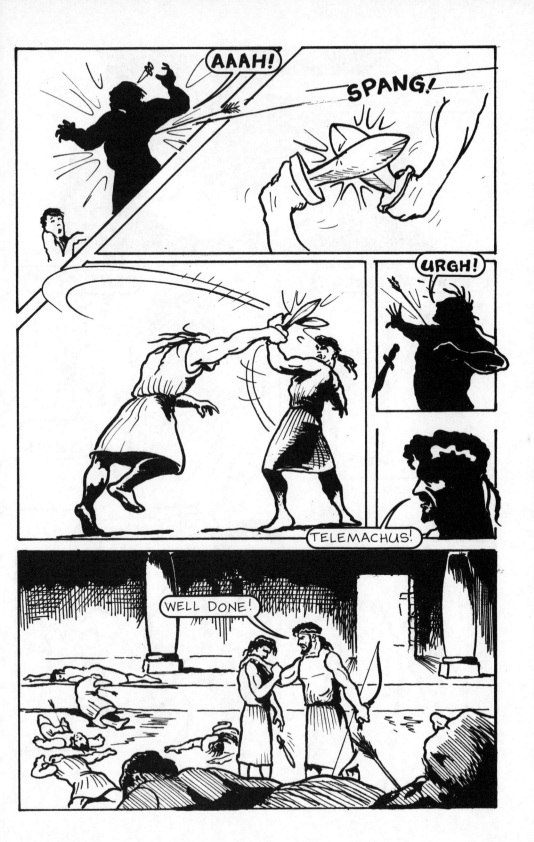